INKFIRE CREATIVE PUBLISHING PRESENTS:

FANTASY WRITING PROMPTS

200 Sparks to Ignite Worlds of Magic and Imagination

InkFire

Spark your stories

First Edition - 2025

ISBN: 979-8-9938345-0-4
Printed in the United States by Amazon KDP
InkFire Creative Publishing
Binghamton, NY
Spark Your Stories

For the storytellers who look beyond the veil, who find

magic in the quiet places and light in the dark. This

book is for you.

Every story begins with a single spark.

Welcome to Fantasy Writing Prompts – A collection designed to awaken imagination and guide your creative fire. Within these pages, you'll find ideas that challenge the boundaries of what worlds can be, questions that beg to be answered, and whispers of magic waiting for a voice.

At InkFire Creative Publishing, we believe every story holds the power to transform, to connect, and to endure. May these prompts light the path toward worlds yet unseen and characters yet unimagined.

Let your light burn bright.

- InkFire Creative Publishing

WORLD SPARK PROMPTS

Ideas that shape realms, history, and the magic that binds them. The world begins, one spark of imagination at a time.

- *Every world begins with a question no one thought to ask.*

Fantasy Writing Prompt #1

A kingdom floats above the clouds, tethered to the earth by a single chain that is beginning to rust. What happens if it breaks free?

InkFire

Spark your stories

Fantasy Writing Prompt #2

Every river glows blue beneath the moon, and no one remembers why. One night, the glow fades completely.

InkFire

Spark your stories

Fantasy Writing Prompt #3

A forest moves 1 mile west every full moon, swallowing villages and leaving empty plains behind. What is causing this phenomenon and how do the villagers fight back?

InkFire

Spark your stories

Fantasy Writing Prompt #4

The stars are arranged in runes, spelling out messages that predict disasters, but only one astronomer can read them.

InkFire

Spark your stories

Fantasy Writing Prompt #5

In the center of the desert lies a perfect circle of rain, where time moves slower than everywhere else. How is this possible, and who is in charge?

InkFire
Spark your stories

Fantasy Writing Prompt #6

The gods have abandoned the world, but their temples still whisper prayers when storms roll in.

InkFire

Spark your stories

Fantasy Writing Prompt #7

A great library sunk beneath a lake, and those who dive for its books sometimes return with memories that are not their own.

InkFire

Spark your stories

Fantasy Writing Prompt #8

A city is carved entirely from dragon bone. When danger approaches, the walls hum with warning

Fantasy Writing Prompt #9

The sea turned to glass overnight, trapping ships mid-sail and freezing fish in place. Now people can walk across it to find out what lies beyond.

InkFire

Spark your stories

Fantasy Writing Prompt #10

An eternal blizzard hides a colossal creature whose dreams
cause the storm itself. Someone dug too far and woke it up.

Fantasy Writing Prompt #11

The sun fails to rise once every century, casting the realm into darkness. That single day decides who will rule the next 100 years.

InkFire

Spark your stories

Fantasy Writing Prompt #12

A kingdom's wealth lies in captured lightning, harvested in glass spheres and traded like gold.

InkFire

Spark your stories

Fantasy Writing Prompt #13

A race of mountain dwellers craft music from echoes from the caves they live in, shaping entire songs from the voices of their ancestors.

InkFire

Spark your stories

Fantasy Writing Prompt #14

A moonlit bridge appears only to the dying, leading to somewhere no one has ever described.

InkFire

Spark your stories

Fantasy Writing Prompt #15

Cities grow on the backs of giants who wander oceans so vast that they circle the world. When they collide, mass destruction follows.

InkFire

Spark your stories

Fantasy Writing Prompt #16

A field of statues stand silent, each depicting someone still alive somewhere else. Vandals just knocked one over.

InkFire

Spark your stories

Fantasy Writing Prompt #17

The Northern Lights are actually spirits migrating. One year they decide not to turn north. What happened when the spirits flew south.

Fantasy Writing Prompt #18

A volcano breathes like a sleeping animal, and people live on its slopes, whispering lullabies to keep it calm.

InkFire

Spark your stories

Fantasy Writing Prompt #19

At the edge of the world, waterfalls tumble into an endless storm. No explorer has been willing to get close enough to study its wonders... until now.

InkFire

Spark your stories

Fantasy Writing Prompt #20

The sky once had two suns, and the ruins of the second hang spinning across the heavens.

InkFire

Spark your stories

Fantasy Writing Prompt #21

The capital city rotates slowly, facing a new direction each dawn. Once morning it doesn't move at all and the realm is sent into a frenzy.

InkFire
Spark your stories

Fantasy Writing Prompt #22

A rain of black petals marks the death of a god somewhere in the world.

InkFire

Spark your stories

Fantasy Writing Prompt #23

Every person has a visible thread of fate, able to be read by anyone in the world. That is until a child is born without one.

InkFire

Spark your stories

Fantasy Writing Prompt #24

The ocean whispers names of sailors, promising them treasure in exchange for their memories.

InkFire

Spark your stories

Fantasy Writing Prompt #25

In the deep caverns below, crystal creatures mine their own kind to forge weapons for the surface wars. What happens when they emerge?

InkFire

Spark your stories

Fantasy Writing Prompt #26

A city's shadow moves independently, revealing what its citizens refuse to see

InkFire

Spark your stories

Fantasy Writing Prompt #27

An ancient tower appears in every legend, yet maps show it constantly changes location. A young girl just found it in the woods behind her family's farm.

Fantasy Writing Prompt #28

Once a year, a portal opens in the middle of a crowded
market, and one random person vanishes through it.

Fantasy Writing Prompt #29

Every dream a child has becomes reality, and the kingdom is now tasked to prepare for a war. How do they prepare for to defend against what is to come?

InkFire

Spark your stories

Fantasy Writing Prompt #30

The royal family's blood glows faintly, and rebels have learned how to fake it.

InkFire

Spark your stories

Fantasy Writing Prompt #31

The moon cracked centuries ago and people now mine the fragments that have fallen to the surface. The fragments give strange anti-gravity effects to the beholder.

Fantasy Writing Prompt #32

A city built around a sleeping dragon's heart uses its pulse for endless power.

InkFire

Spark your stories

Fantasy Writing Prompt #33

A desert caravan discovers a living forest, growing overnight from seeds that weren't there the day before. And it is expanding.

InkFire

Spark your stories

Fantasy Writing Prompt #34

When it rains, ghosts appear, repeating the last moments of their lives until the clouds clear.

InkFire

Spark your stories

Fantasy Writing Prompt #35

Every century, the sea delivers a message in a bottle, written
in a language that no one alive can read. This time, the
bottle is held within the grasp of a mermaid.

InkFire

Spark your stories

Fantasy Writing Prompt #36

The wind carries voices of the dead, but only children can hear them clearly.

InkFire

Spark your stories

Fantasy Writing Prompt #37

A star fell to earth, and the first person to touch it becomes the center of a new religion. This cult begins it's journey to take over the world.

InkFire

Spark your stories

Fantasy Writing Prompt #38

A city sits between two realities, and citizens sometimes forget which one they belong to.

InkFire

Spark your stories

Fantasy Writing Prompt #39

A mountain splits open, revealing an entire civilization that evolved underground for millennia. They did not want to be found like this.

InkFire

Spark your stories

Fantasy Writing Prompt #40

The kingdoms calendar reset to zero, and everyone forgets what year it was before.

InkFire

Spark your stories

Fantasy Writing Prompt #41

A bridge stretches over an abys that hums, and travelers who cross it claim they can hear songs from another world. An accident just sent a group tumbling over the edge.

Fantasy Writing Prompt #42

The rain never falls in one village, but their crops thrive anyway, nourished by something unseen.

InkFire

Spark your stories

Fantasy Writing Prompt #43

An eclipse lasts 3 days casting the world into darkness.
When the dawn finally comes again, things are different and
the usual way of things is changed.

Fantasy Writing Prompt #44

A river flows uphill, carrying messages from a deep sea dwelling society.

InkFire

Spark your stories

Fantasy Writing Prompt #45

A city's buildings rearrange themselves every decade, and no one can remember the old street layouts. This messes with economy, politics and the order of things.

InkFire

Spark your stories

Fantasy Writing Prompt #46

Ancient statues are bleeding, and scholars argue if it is a miracle or an omen.

InkFire

Spark your stories

Fantasy Writing Prompt #47

The moonlight turns everything it touches to silver for a single year. The thieves plan their grand heists then. The economy is thrown when the silver disappears.

Fantasy Writing Prompt #48

Every shadow in the empire freezes at noon while everything else keeps moving. What is happening?

InkFire

Spark your stories

Fantasy Writing Prompt #49

The world ends every thousand years, only to restart slightly different each time. One person remembers all of the previous versions.

InkFire

Spark your stories

Fantasy Writing Prompt #50

Beneath a kingdom's castle lies a heart that beats. When it stops, the land above will die.

Fantasy Writing Prompt #51

A kingdom's sky turns crimson out of nowhere with no warning. It lasts one night, and anyone born beneath it is said to be cursed.

InkFire

Spark your stories

Fantasy Writing Prompt #52

The moon's reflection reveals hidden cities that don't exist in the daylight.

InkFire

Spark your stories

Fantasy Writing Prompt #53

An island drifts freely across the ocean, appearing at random coasts and inhabited by new people each time. The island is just the top of a roaming ship with its own civilization.

InkFire

Spark your stories

Fantasy Writing Prompt #54

The mountains begin to sing with an ominous warning of what is to come.

InkFire

Spark your stories

Fantasy Writing Prompt #55

A city's ruler is chosen by a mythical beast who appears to the worthy. But the creature has not come for decades to select a new leader.

InkFire

Spark your stories

Fantasy Writing Prompt #56

In the center of the citadel, an enormous hourglass runs
backwards. Nobody knows what the countdown is for.

InkFire

Spark your stories

Fantasy Writing Prompt #57

A valley where mirrors grow like wildflowers, each reflection shows the true person's soul. It is hard hiding from them but most people try.

InkFire

Spark your stories

Fantasy Writing Prompt #58

A colossal tree connects all realms. The lowest branch finally falls to touch earth.

InkFire

Spark your stories

Fantasy Writing Prompt #59

Deep beneath the ocean, explorers find the ruins of a
floating city that has died and sunk to the bottom. It is
perfectly preserved and still glowing with light.

InkFire

Spark your stories

Fantasy Writing Prompt #60

A priest claims that the sun is being devoured by something unseen. No one believes him until the light starts to go out.

InkFire

Spark your stories

CHARACTER DRIVEN HOOKS

ideas that breathe life into heroes, villains, and everyone in between. Stories live through the hearts that carry them.

- Every legend begins with someone brave enough to change.

Fantasy Writing Prompt #61

You awaken on a castle thrown and everyone is kneeling before you, calling you by a name that you do not know.

InkFire

Spark your stories

Fantasy Writing Prompt #62

You've spent your life slaying monsters, but one begs for mercy using your mothers voice.

InkFire

Spark your stories

Fantasy Writing Prompt #63

A thief steals from the gods and finds a divine spark burning in their chest.

InkFire

Spark your stories

Fantasy Writing Prompt #64

You inherit a sword that whispers your families' secrets as you wield it.

InkFire

Spark your stories

Fantasy Writing Prompt #65

A scholar deciphers an ancient prophecy only to find their own name as the final word.

InkFire

Spark your stories

Fantasy Writing Prompt #66

Your twin was executed years ago. You catch glimpses of them in the crowd during a festival.

Fantasy Writing Prompt #67

You're cursed to feel the emotions of everyone you meet, and today, someone near you feels murderous.

InkFire

Spark your stories

Fantasy Writing Prompt #68

The queen asks you to assassinate her. Your reward, she promises you the throne afterward.

InkFire

Spark your stories

Fantasy Writing Prompt #69

You were born with wings that must remain hidden. Today,
the wind refuses to obey.

Fantasy Writing Prompt #70

You find your reflection missing from every mirror, and soon people stop recognizing you.

Fantasy Writing Prompt #71

You're the bodyguard of a child prophesied to end the world, and they've just asked you if you believe in fate.

Fantasy Writing Prompt #72

A knight returns home to find everyone convinced they've never existed.

InkFire

Spark your stories

Fantasy Writing Prompt #73

You wake up in your enemy's body the morning of your final battle.

InkFire

Spark your stories

Fantasy Writing Prompt #74

You were raised by dragons and must now hide among humans who fear them.

Fantasy Writing Prompt #75

A healer discovers that every life they save steals time from their own.

Fantasy Writing Prompt #76

You dream of a stranger every night — until one day, you meet them alive and terrified.

InkFire

Spark your stories

Fantasy Writing Prompt #77

A ghost chooses you as their voice in the mortal world, but they only speak in riddles.

Fantasy Writing Prompt #78

You're destined to wear the crown, but every step closer makes the kingdom fall further into ruin.

InkFire

Spark your stories

Fantasy Writing Prompt #79

You hear your name in the prayers of thousands — though you've never been a god.

InkFire

Spark your stories

Fantasy Writing Prompt #80

The kingdom celebrates you as its hero, but you remember dying in that war.

InkFire

Spark your stories

Fantasy Writing Prompt #81

You find a letter written in your handwriting — dated fifty years in the future.

InkFire
Spark your stories

Fantasy Writing Prompt #82

You can read minds, but only when someone lies. It is getting pretty darn loud in your head.

InkFire

Spark your stories

Fantasy Writing Prompt #83

You're cursed to relive your worst day every time you speak it aloud.

InkFire

Spark your stories

Fantasy Writing Prompt #84

You find your true love's name written on your sword — and it's someone you've sworn to kill.

InkFire

Spark your stories

Fantasy Writing Prompt #85

You're the only one who can see the invisible crown
hovering above the tyrant's head.

InkFire

Spark your stories

Fantasy Writing Prompt #86

You were born with a pink shadow. Hiding from the enemy forces is difficult, but you make the best of it.

Fantasy Writing Prompt #87

A stranger hands you a key that opens any lock, including the ones in your memory.

InkFire

Spark your stories

Fantasy Writing Prompt #88

You've lived a thousand lives, but this time, the person you love remembers you too, and what you did.

InkFire

Spark your stories

Fantasy Writing Prompt #89

You discover you are the villain of every legend your people tell. Everyone seems to be connecting the dots too.

Fantasy Writing Prompt #90

You are a dragon trapped in human form, and the spell begins to fade.

InkFire

Spark your stories

Fantasy Writing Prompt #91

You find a book that writes your story a day ahead of time.
You wake up one morning and find the ink has stopped.

InkFire

Spark your stories

Fantasy Writing Prompt #92

You were promised eternal life but awaken after centuries to find everyone immortal but you.

InkFire

Spark your stories

Fantasy Writing Prompt #93

You're the last of your kind, and the gods have sent you a
dream offering a choice: rebirth or revenge.

InkFire

Spark your stories

Fantasy Writing Prompt #94

You can steal memories — and someone offers you an empire in exchange for their guilt.

InkFire

Spark your stories

Fantasy Writing Prompt #95

You fall in love with the person meant to kill you to fulfill their prophecy. Are they using love to get close?

InkFire

Spark your stories

Fantasy Writing Prompt #96

You return home to find the stars rearranged into your
family's sigil. What comes next is fascinating.

InkFire

Spark your stories

Fantasy Writing Prompt #97

You are a seer who can no longer tell the future — because it's already been written by you.

InkFire

Spark your stories

Fantasy Writing Prompt #98

You uncover a painting of yourself, centuries old, holding a
child who looks like your twin.

InkFire

Spark your stories

Fantasy Writing Prompt #99

You're chosen as a vessel for an ancient spirit — and it starts whispering doubts about your own life.

InkFire

Spark your stories

Fantasy Writing Prompt #100

You once saved the world; now it must be saved from you.
Power and fame have gone to your mind. Is it too late?

InkFire

Spark your stories

Fantasy Writing Prompt #101

You awaken in a realm built entirely from your dreams. The nightmares are starting to wake up.

InkFire

Spark your stories

Fantasy Writing Prompt #102

You are a bard who can sing the dead back to life, but each
song erases one of your memories.

InkFire

Spark your stories

Fantasy Writing Prompt #103

You see glowing marks on people destined to die soon, and your own marks begin to flicker.

Fantasy Writing Prompt #104

A gate to an unknown realm arrived long ago. You are one of the guards. You begin to question why it needs guarding.

InkFire

Spark your stories

Fantasy Writing Prompt #105

You're a soldier in a war no one recalls starting, but your enemy insists you fought side by side once.

InkFire

Spark your stories

Fantasy Writing Prompt #106

You inherit a cursed crown that speaks in the voices of past
rulers. Everything isn't as it seems though.

InkFire

Spark your stories

Fantasy Writing Prompt #107

You've been imprisoned for crimes you haven't committed... yet.

InkFire

Spark your stories

Fantasy Writing Prompt #108

Your bloodline is blessed by the gods, but you're the first to renounce them for what they've done.

Fantasy Writing Prompt #109

You wake up to find every color missing from the world
except yellow. Why?

InkFire

Spark your stories

Fantasy Writing Prompt #110

You discover your tears turn to gemstones, and someone will kill for them.

Fantasy Writing Prompt #111

You've sworn to protect a secret that could destroy the world, but today you forget what it is.

InkFire

Spark your stories

Fantasy Writing Prompt #112

You return to your childhood village and find everyone still the same age, except you. Your friends don't recognize you.

InkFire

Spark your stories

Fantasy Writing Prompt #113

You awaken on a castle throne and everyone is kneeling before you, calling you by a name that you do not know.

Fantasy Writing Prompt #114

A mark on your wrist burns whenever someone speaks a lie near you.

InkFire

Spark your stories

You've dreamed of a door that hasn't been found, until you go on a hike with some friends from the village.

Fantasy Writing Prompt #116

You can speak with your future self through reflections.
There is lots of fire and smoke in the background.

Fantasy Writing Prompt #117

You carry a lantern that reveals thieves in the night.
Tonight, the light shines upon you.

InkFire

Spark your stories

Fantasy Writing Prompt #118

You make a wish never to be forgotten. Now you can't die
and you live as an outcast in the hills.

InkFire

Spark your stories

Fantasy Writing Prompt #119

You are a monster hunter who was stung by his prey. There is a change happening within your body.

InkFire

Spark your stories

Fantasy Writing Prompt #120

You receive a letter from your future child, begging you not to meet their mother.

InkFire

Spark your stories

You have squandered a thousand lives. Now you need to fix what you have done with this one before it is too late.

You find a crown buried under your flower bed. Now everyone magically remembers you as the ruler.

Fantasy Writing Prompt #123

You wake up covered in ash surrounded by thousands of soldiers. They are chanting Phoenix and hoisting you up.

InkFire

Spark your stories

Fantasy Writing Prompt #124

You can summon any creature by drawing it. You are running out of eraser though and they begin to stick around.

InkFire

Spark your stories

Fantasy Writing Prompt #125

Your name has been erased from record and nobody can say it now. You wander namelessly through life until…

InkFire

Spark your stories

Fantasy Writing Prompt #126

You are the apprentice of death. You cope with your job,
until death wakes you up in the middle of the night.

Fantasy Writing Prompt #127

You meet the version of yourself that has lived life with no regrets. It is almost unbearable.

InkFire

Spark your stories

Fantasy Writing Prompt #128

**You have convinced the gods that you are one of them.
Now you are selected as a champion, to fight another god.**

Fantasy Writing Prompt #129

You find a dagger that glows green to the rhythm of your heartbeat. Well, red during battle.

Fantasy Writing Prompt #130

You are the only person who can see wings on people destined to die soon.

InkFire

Spark your stories

PLOT PROBLEM PROMPTS

Conflicts, twists, and challenges to drive your stories forward. When the world breaks, stories are born.

- Without conflict, there is no creation.

Fantasy Writing Prompt #131

A royal wedding is interrupted when both brides claim to be the same person.

InkFire

Spark your stories

Fantasy Writing Prompt #132

A storm refuses to leave one city, and the rain starts whispering people's secrets.

InkFire

Spark your stories

Fantasy Writing Prompt #133

A caravan disappears between two towns, but no one has any record of it ever existing.

InkFire

Spark your stories

Fantasy Writing Prompt #134

The king's treasure has been stolen, and in its place lies a sleeping child made of gold.

Fantasy Writing Prompt #135

A magical plague created to spread laughter turns deadly when it stops.

InkFire

Spark your stories

Fantasy Writing Prompt #136

**The prophecy meant to save the world has been
mistranslated for centuries.**

Fantasy Writing Prompt #137

A warlord gains immortality, but only if their army keeps on winning the war.

InkFire

Spark your stories

Fantasy Writing Prompt #138

The kingdom's greatest hero, long dead with statues to prove it, shows up at the gate, very undead.

InkFire

Spark your stories

Fantasy Writing Prompt #139

A thief steals the moon little by little. The nights grow darker each day.

InkFire

Spark your stories

Fantasy Writing Prompt #140

The world lay in ruin. The gods demand a new world to
replace the old one. Heroes must step up to rebuild it.

Fantasy Writing Prompt #141

A tornado with magical powers rearranges the city, families and social standings. No one remembers but a select few.

InkFire

Spark your stories

Fantasy Writing Prompt #142

A cult worships an imprisoned demon. Now the demon has disappeared, but the cult remains.

Fantasy Writing Prompt #143

A magical ink rewrites history whenever it is used to write on the scrolls. It pays to be a librarian in times like these.

InkFire

Spark your stories

Fantasy Writing Prompt #144

A bridge collapses between realms, trapping travelers in both worlds.

InkFire

Spark your stories

Fantasy Writing Prompt #145

A chosen one refuses their destiny. The prophecy rewrites itself and now you are the one to deliver.

InkFire

Spark your stories

Fantasy Writing Prompt #146

A clock maker builds a device that counts down to the end
of magic. What would you do with the time you have left?

Fantasy Writing Prompt #147

An army shows up at the gates under a flag that no one has ever seen before, and the citadel is not ready.

InkFire

Spark your stories

Fantasy Writing Prompt #148

A mysterious sickness turns people to stone. The only thing is, their eyes still move and show intelligence.

Fantasy Writing Prompt #149

One star vanishes per night. At first nobody understands...
until they do. What happens when the last one goes out?

InkFire

Spark your stories

Fantasy Writing Prompt #150

The god's temples start bleeding, and prayers begin to fall on deaf ears. Someone needs to find out what is going on.

InkFire

Spark your stories

Fantasy Writing Prompt #151

**A crown forged by dragon fire corrupts whomever wears it.
Kings have gone mad for ages. Who will break the cycle?**

InkFire

Spark your stories

Fantasy Writing Prompt #152

The dead refuse to stay buried, demanding justice for long forgotten crimes.

InkFire

Spark your stories

Fantasy Writing Prompt #153

A realm's borders shift overnight and entire kingdoms have vanished from the maps.

InkFire

Spark your stories

Fantasy Writing Prompt #154

A spell has gone wrong and now a soul has been split into two bodies. They cannot live apart.

InkFire

Spark your stories

Fantasy Writing Prompt #155

A storm has shipwrecked travelers on an island that should not exist. There are strange things happening.

InkFire

Spark your stories

Fantasy Writing Prompt #156

A kingdom's ruler has disappeared and is replaced by a shadow ruling in his stead. He looks just like the other guy.

InkFire

Spark your stories

Fantasy Writing Prompt #157

A massive door rises from the ground, locked from the inside. Years go by until someone finds a way in.

InkFire

Spark your stories

Fantasy Writing Prompt #158

Children born under a crimson moon are taken from their homes and delivered as offerings to the gods.

Fantasy Writing Prompt #159

A warrior wakes after a battle won. He was the hero, but someone else has taken the credit.

Fantasy Writing Prompt #160

A war breaks out between those who wield magic, and those
who dream to capture it.

InkFire

Spark your stories

Fantasy Writing Prompt #161

A letter arrives claiming your entire reality is a story, and the author is dying.

InkFire

Spark your stories

Fantasy Writing Prompt #162

An entire village sleeps for years, only waking when someone tries to move in.

InkFire

Spark your stories

Fantasy Writing Prompt #163

The ocean starts to recede, revealing ruins of a civilization that shouldn't exist.

Fantasy Writing Prompt #164

An unbreakable sword is dropped during battle. It is picked up by thieves only to reveal its true power.

InkFire

Spark your stories

Fantasy Writing Prompt #165

The seasons stop changing and farmers find frost growing up from the soil. What is causing the cold?

Fantasy Writing Prompt #166

A magical book is found tucked deep in the stacks of a library. What type of magic is given to the reader?

Fantasy Writing Prompt #167

Every time magic is used, someone disappears from the realm at random.

InkFire

Spark your stories

Fantasy Writing Prompt #168

A kingdom has been plagued and all people infected lose ability to speak.

Fantasy Writing Prompt #169

The night sky cracks open after an asteroid rips through the
atmosphere. Eyes are watching from the beyond.

InkFire

Spark your stories

Fantasy Writing Prompt #170

A competition decides the next leader. The entrants include you, a few other humans and many creatures not fit to rule.

Fantasy Writing Prompt #171

The sun has burned out. Now the people must learn how to live in the cold and dark.

InkFire

Spark your stories

Fantasy Writing Prompt #172

A city built out of gold, abandoned for centuries, has a thief problem. They mine gold and sell it. Then they get sick.

InkFire

Spark your stories

Fantasy Writing Prompt #173

A mirror obtained by a traveling merchant shows the beholder choices that they didn't make.

InkFire

Spark your stories

Fantasy Writing Prompt #174

An immortal sorcerer's heart is split into shards and thrust inside of five regular humans.

InkFire

Spark your stories

Fantasy Writing Prompt #175

A mysterious ship sails into port with no visible crew. Only eerie music echoing from below deck.

InkFire

Spark your stories

Fantasy Writing Prompt #176

An oracle starts speaking nonsense until all of it comes together, and prophecies begin to come true.

Fantasy Writing Prompt #177

**Every newborn child is branded with the mark of the clan.
Some defect. They are called the re-branded.**

InkFire

Spark your stories

Fantasy Writing Prompt #178

An ancient guardian made from stone, thought to protect the realm wakes. He attacks instead.

Fantasy Writing Prompt #179

**A mage makes his enemies weapons attack their wielders.
Someone more powerful comes along and does it to him.**

Fantasy Writing Prompt #180

**The gods declare a year of silence. Anybody who speaks is
cursed instantly.**

Fantasy Writing Prompt #181

A city was wiped out overnight. Merchants and curriers find nothing but sand.

InkFire

Spark your stories

Fantasy Writing Prompt #182

A tower rises every dawn and crumbles each night. It gets
taller each time. Runners are sent to get the loot at the top.

InkFire

Spark your stories

Fantasy Writing Prompt #183

Part of the moon falls into the sea. A major tsunami wipes out the coastal economy. The highlands become powerful.

InkFire

Spark your stories

Fantasy Writing Prompt #184

The final dragon dies, but the skies begin to burn anyway as the gods are upset.

Fantasy Writing Prompt #185

A magical portal opens but only the children can pass through without harm.

Fantasy Writing Prompt #186

The dead begin to send letters to the living, dropping them off on the doorstep of their old dwellings.

Fantasy Writing Prompt #187

A long sleep plagues a city, but when they awake, all wishes come true.

InkFire

Spark your stories

Fantasy Writing Prompt #188

A kingdom is frozen mid-battle except for one warrior. He must decide what comes next. Take out the enemy or flee.

InkFire

Spark your stories

Fantasy Writing Prompt #189

Sea monsters begin to evolve. They grow legs and can breathe on land. This is about to get interesting.

InkFire

Spark your stories

Fantasy Writing Prompt #190

A forgotten god awakes in the body of a normal peasant man who works in the forges.

InkFire

Spark your stories

Fantasy Writing Prompt #191

A city returns to glory on the coattails of a new religion that has formed. As it spreads, the power grows.

InkFire

Spark your stories

Fantasy Writing Prompt #192

The worlds last mage discovers that his powers are killing the planet.

InkFire

Spark your stories

Fantasy Writing Prompt #193

A rift opens in the sky, and the rain begins to burn flesh.
Weather predictions pay well in times such as these.

InkFire

Spark your stories

Fantasy Writing Prompt #194

The oldest tree know to man dies, and funny things begin to happen around the kingdom.

Fantasy Writing Prompt #195

The kingdom's music stops and even the birds fall silent.
Bards are looking for new jobs.

InkFire

Spark your stories

Fantasy Writing Prompt #196

Caves on the outskirts of the citadel begin to flow with a golden magma. When it cools, what do the people find?

Fantasy Writing Prompt #197

The last prophecy burns itself away, leaving only your name.
no one can remember what it said but they all look to you.

InkFire

Spark your stories

Fantasy Writing Prompt #198

The world begins to unravel. People start to catch on that it is your fault.

InkFire

Spark your stories

Fantasy Writing Prompt #199

A plague rips through the land, causing the sick to run
everywhere until exhaustion takes over.

InkFire

Spark your stories

Fantasy Writing Prompt #200

A tournament, fought to the death, is played for the citizens entertainment. Your name was drawn.

At InkFire Creative Publishing, we believe every writer carries a spark of imagination capable of lighting entire worlds.

Our mission is to help that spark grow, igniting creativity, nurturing passion for storytelling, and craft beautiful tools that guide writers toward their own world of wonder.

From prompts to projects, from a single line to a bound book, InkFire exists to remind you that every story begins with one glowing ember of inspiration.

InkFire

Spark your stories

Matthew Rowe is an engineer, a creative mind, and a lifelong storyteller. With a passion for creativity, structure, and the magic of imagination, he founded **InkFire Creative Publishing** as a home for tools that inspire and challenge writers to build worlds of their own.

When he is not designing or writing, Matthew enjoys exploring stories in every form, from novels and games — to art and animation — always searching for the next spark of an idea waiting to catch flame.

Follow InkFire Creative Publishing online to stay connected for future releases, guides, and creative tools.

Every story begins with a spark.

Thank you for letting InkFire be a part of your creative journey.
Your imagination fuels worlds, builds legends, and keeps the fire
of *storytelling alive.*

May the words you write here grow into something greater — a
world that only you could bring to life.

Keep creating. Keep Dreaming. Keep your spark alive.

www.ingramcontent.com/pod-product-compliance
Lightning Source LLC
Chambersburg PA
CBHW070746180626
46818CB00007B/3012